Robert Louis Stevenson
(1850-1894)
was born in Edinburgh,
Scotland.

Treasure Island was first
published in 1883.

© 1993 Twin Books Ltd

Produced by
TWIN BOOKS LTD
Kimbolton House
117A Fulham Road
London SW3 6RL
England

Directed by CND – Muriel Nathan-Deiller
Illustrated by Van Gool-Lefèvre-Loiseaux
Text adapted by Sue Jackson

ISBN: 1 85469 918 0

Printed in Hong Kong

This edition printed 1994

Treasure Island

TWIN BOOKS

Chapter 1
THE OLD SEA-DOG

My father owned an old tavern called the Admiral Benbow. It had been built many years ago near a creek, and was often said to be a landmark for smugglers. One day, an old seaman with a scarred face arrived at the inn looking for lodgings. He found the place to his liking and quickly settled in.

The Captain, as we soon named him, spent his days on the cliffs looking out to sea, his telescope scanning the horizon.

The old sea-dog was not good company, and often seemed irritable and anxious. He drank large quantities of rum every evening, and told wild tales of swashbuckling pirates and their adventures on the high seas, which disturbed our other customers.

One morning in January, a disreputable-looking stranger appeared at the inn.

"Is my pal, Bill, here?" he asked. I told him that our only guest was the Captain.

"That must be him," replied the man. "Has he a scar on his right cheek?" When I confirmed that he had, the man sat down at a table. "I'll wait for him here then," he said. "Bill *will be* pleased to see me." The Captain, however, on his return did not appear delighted to see his visitor. "Black Dog! You wretched scoundrel," he scowled. "What are you doing here?"

The two men retired to the Captain's rooms. I heard raised voices, and soon they were shouting. A fight broke out. Suddenly, Black Dog, his shoulder bleeding, ran down the stairs and out of the inn. The Captain chased after him, but Black Dog managed to escape.

One evening, when the Captain was drunk, he spoke of an old buccaneer called Flint, of a secret, the black spot and the precious contents of his sea chest. He kept mumbling "pieces of gold". His story made little sense, and I was only half listening as my father, who had been ill for some time, was dying.

The day after my poor father's funeral, a blind beggar passed the inn. He had a long stick and his sailor's coat was in rags. He was looking for "Billy Bones". When the Captain returned from his daily walk, the blind man handed him a square of paper, then left. The paper was marked on one side.

"The black spot!" gasped the Captain. He was terrified. He read the note, turned blue in the face, choked and fell to the floor. He was dead within seconds. I picked up the note. On it was scrawled just one sentence: "You have until ten o'clock tonight."

My mother came running in. The Captain owed us money. If the others were going to return tonight, we had to move quickly. Trembling, I took the key from the chain around the Captain's neck and unlocked his sea chest. Inside, I found a small bag of gold coins and some papers in an oilskin packet. My mother started counting the money, when we heard the blind man's stick tapping on the frozen ground. It was followed by the sound of many footsteps. I grabbed the packet, and we hurriedly left the inn. We had just enough time to hide ourselves under the arch of a nearby bridge before they arrived!

By the light of their lantern we saw seven or eight seamen rush into the tavern. One of their number was Black Dog! It was not long before they came running out, and I heard the blind man cry, "Damn that boy! He has taken Flint's papers! Find him, quickly! He can't have gone far."

My mother was terrified, and I was shaking with fright. Suddenly, we heard a sharp whistle and the sound of horses' hooves. The customs men, hunting smugglers, were going to save us! The villains panicked and fled, abandoning the blind man. In the confusion, he fell to the ground and was trampled to death by the approaching horses.

We'd had a narrow escape! I thanked the customs men warmly, and then went in search of Doctor Livesey.

Doctor Livesey was with the local squire, Mr. Trelawney. I told them about the Captain's sudden death and the raid on the inn. Then I handed them the packet I had found in the sea chest. They had both heard the legend of Captain Flint, a bloodthirsty pirate, long since dead. Now his first mate, Billy Bones, had died, leaving behind some papers that his former shipmates were desperate to find!

Squire Trelawney broke open the packet. Among Billy Bones' accounts was a badly drawn map of an island, on which there were some roughly sketched landmarks, and a red cross. "These are directions to Flint's treasure," declared Trelawney. "We *must* recover it!"

Within a few days Trelawney had left for Bristol, where he hired a ship and crew for the voyage. Livesey was to be the ship's doctor and I, Jim Hawkins, the cabin boy. I was delighted. I was being offered the adventure of a lifetime!

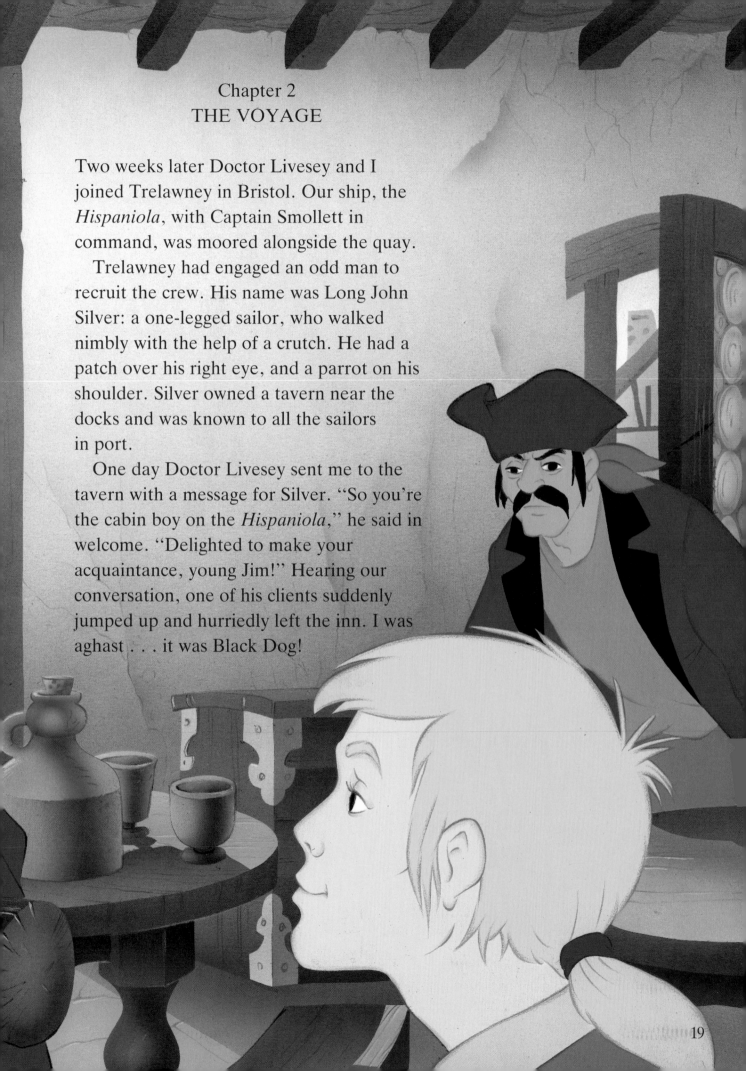

Chapter 2
THE VOYAGE

Two weeks later Doctor Livesey and I joined Trelawney in Bristol. Our ship, the *Hispaniola*, with Captain Smollett in command, was moored alongside the quay.

Trelawney had engaged an odd man to recruit the crew. His name was Long John Silver: a one-legged sailor, who walked nimbly with the help of a crutch. He had a patch over his right eye, and a parrot on his shoulder. Silver owned a tavern near the docks and was known to all the sailors in port.

One day Doctor Livesey sent me to the tavern with a message for Silver. "So you're the cabin boy on the *Hispaniola*," he said in welcome. "Delighted to make your acquaintance, young Jim!" Hearing our conversation, one of his clients suddenly jumped up and hurriedly left the inn. I was aghast . . . it was Black Dog!

"I've never met that man before," Long John Silver assured me, when I questioned him. He also recounted the incident to Livesey and Trelawney. I relaxed. Silver appeared to be honest and trustworthy, so I put the incident out of my mind.

The next day we embarked. Captain Smollett was suspicious of the crew. He insisted that the gunpowder and firearms be stored near our cabins in case of mutiny.

"I didn't recruit these men, and so cannot vouch for their honesty," he told Trelawney crossly. "And, you've mentioned the word 'treasure' far too often. The crew can think of nothing else!" Trelawney protested in vain. We all knew that the squire was incorrigibly talkative!

Despite Smollett's fears, the journey began well. The *Hispaniola* was an excellent sailing vessel and her crew worked hard.

Long John Silver had appointed himself ship's cook. However, it soon became clear that the sailors obeyed him as if he was the master of the ship.

I also noticed that they often sang a sinister sea shanty – one that Captain Bill had chorused when drunk at my father's tavern:

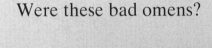

Fifteen men on the dead man's chest
Yo, ho, ho, and a bottle of rum!
Drink and the devil have done for the rest
Yo, ho, ho and a bottle of rum!

This song always sent shivers down my spine. Silver's parrot, an evil green bird, named "Captain Flint" after the famous buccaneer, often screeched between foul curses, "Pieces of gold!" I couldn't help thinking about the gold coins in Captain Bill's sea chest.

Were these bad omens?

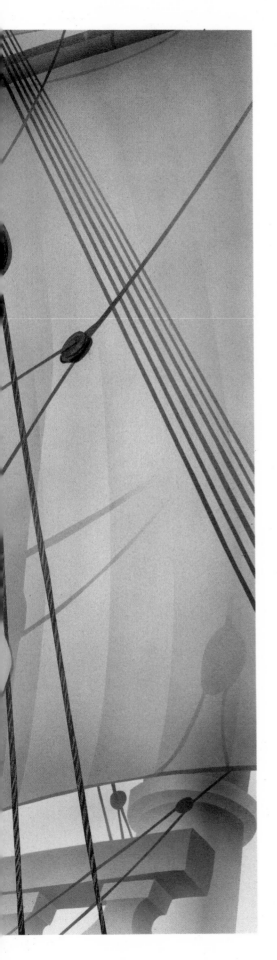

One evening, I went to fetch an apple from the barrel on the bridge. When we had started our journey the barrel had been full. Now it was almost empty and I had to climb in to retrieve one. Once inside I could not be seen, and before I could clamber out, I heard footsteps approaching. Long John Silver was talking to one of the sailors, "Most of the crew have joined me. Here's the plan: we'll let Smollett and Trelawney find the treasure – after all, they have the map. Once it has been loaded aboard, we'll kill them and seize the ship. Then the treasure will be ours!"

The sailor hesitated. I recoiled, terrified, inside the barrel while they discussed the plan further. At last, they moved away and I was able to leave my hiding place.

At that very moment, the sailor on watch cried out, "Land, ho!" After months at sea, we had finally arrived at Treasure Island.

The ship was anchored in a small cove on the south side of the island. Once the initial excitement had died down, I ran to tell Doctor Livesey about Long John Silver's plot. Trelawney and Captain Smollett were with him in his cabin. I repeated the conversation I had unwittingly overheard.

"You were right, Captain Smollett," admitted Trelawney. "I should have been more careful. Now our lives are in danger."

"They won't mutiny until we've found the treasure," replied Smollett reassuringly.

"But Silver, or his sailors, might well change the plan," objected Livesey. "They are all extremely excited."

"Let's run that risk," suggested Trelawney. "In the meantime, we musn't arouse their suspicions."

The next day, a number of the crew, with Silver in command, rowed to the shore. The rest of the ship's company stayed aboard with Smollett, Trelawney and the doctor. I should have stayed behind with them, but was eager to land and explore the island. So, I hid, curled up in a tarpaulin, in the front of one of the boats and managed to get ashore without being discovered.

Chapter 3
THE ABANDONED SAILOR

The island was large and, except for birds and snakes, seemed uninhabited. I thought Long John Silver and his band of sailors were at the other end of the beach when I spotted them. Luckily, I was hidden from view. They were harassing one of the crew, who stubbornly refused to join their mutiny. Long John Silver drew his cutlass and, without a moment's hesitation, murdered the loyal sailor. The other pirates applauded! I was horrified!

Just as Doctor Livesey had feared, the sailors had persuaded Silver to alter his original plan. They were going to mutiny *before* the treasure was found! At all costs, I must return to the ship and warn the others. But the boats were now guarded by one of the mutineers. I fled to avoid the risk of being taken captive.

I was breathless by the time I reached the foot of a small hill. I stopped to rest when, out of nowhere, loomed a tall, bearded man, dressed only in tatters. Shaken by his appearance, I jumped back.

"Don't be afraid!" he said. "I'm Ben Gunn. My companions, the wretches, abandoned me on this island three years ago. I have been totally alone! Please, please, rescue me," he pleaded.

When I'd recovered, I told him about our ship and the mutiny led by Silver.

"Long John Silver!" he exclaimed. "I know the blackguard! He was Flint's quartermaster! For pity's sake, don't tell him I'm here!" He was trembling with fright. I tried to calm him, but he begged to go aboard ship and speak to Squire Trelawney. "I have built a small boat which is hidden on the beach. We'll get it and row out to the *Hispaniola*," he said excitedly.

We heard cannon fire. I was amazed. Why was the *Hispaniola's* cannon firing on the island? What had happened on board ship? In the distance, I could also hear musket shots. Then, I saw our flag, the Union Jack, fluttering above some trees. Ben Gunn looked around. "Someone has hoisted the Jolly Roger on the ship," he said. "Your friends must be taking shelter in the fort.

Flint built a fort on the island," he explained, "when he came to bury his treasure. I was a member of the crew, and Billy Bones was first mate, on that – Flint's last – voyage to the island. He took six men ashore with him to bury the treasure and build the fort. When the men had finished he murdered them so that they could not reveal his secret."

Another cannon shot split the air.

"If Trelawney wants to see me, he'll find me close to the foot of that small hill," shouted Ben Gunn as he fled.

I stumbled towards the fort. With great difficulty, I scaled the stockade and fell into Doctor Livesey's arms.

Once inside the fort, I saw Smollett, Trelawney, Grey the carpenter and the few sailors who'd remained loyal. Doctor Livesey recounted the events which had taken place on the *Hispaniola* since my departure: "Like you," he said, "I also wanted to look around the island. By chance, I found the fort and discovered that it was in a reasonable condition. I'd hardly returned aboard ship when the mutiny broke out. Despite our stock of weapons, we'd have been unable to defend our position for long. We were outnumbered. So, while Smollett and Trelawney held the mutineers at gunpoint, I hurriedly threw some provisions and ammunition into the remaining boat. Then we rowed to the island and took refuge in the fort. By now, Silver will know we are here, and it won't be long before his band of pirates attack us!"

Chapter 4
THE FORT

What were we going to do? The fort was solid, the stockade high and difficult to scale, but for how long could we resist an attack by the mutineers? And then what? The ship was in their hands!

While we were waiting for the attack, and to distract my companions, I told them about my discoveries. Doctor Livesey was particularly interested in my news of Ben Gunn.

The night soon passed. At dawn, Long John Silver appeared, under the protection of a white flag. He had come to bargain with us, and suggested that we give him the map with the directions to the treasure. In return, he would help us leave the island.

"Never!" yelled Smollett.

Silver swore. Then he left, shouting, "In an hour, your fort will be no more. I'll smash it, like an empty rum barrel!"

Before long we heard bloodcurdling cries. The pirates were running towards the fort. The attack had begun! Agile as monkeys, the pirates scaled the parapets and jumped into the enclosure. Soon we were fighting hand to hand.

There were casualties on both sides, when suddenly, exhausted by the assault on the fort and the fighting, the pirates took to their heels.

There were no further attacks that day, and towards midday, Doctor Livesey, the map stuffed in his pocket, took his pistols and left the fort. What madness! Where was he going? Perhaps to find Ben Gunn? I decided to venture out too. When no one was looking I took a pair of pistols, and slipped away. I'd had an idea of my own! I was going to find Ben Gunn's small boat and then . . . .

I searched the beach, taking care not to be seen by the mutineers. The tiny boat was no more than the hollowed out trunk of a pine tree. I dragged it to the water's edge, jumped in and rowed, with all my might, towards the *Hispaniola*.

Night was falling. Fortunately, the wind and the currents helped my course. At last, I arrived close to the ship. Now, I would be able to execute my plan! To prevent the mutineers from escaping in the *Hispaniola* I was going to cut her moorings, let her drift and run her aground on the island. With my knife, I cut one mooring, then another. The ship began to drift . . . out to sea! The waves knocked my small boat against its hull and I only just managed to clamber aboard the *Hispaniola* before the small boat was smashed to pieces.

Chapter 5
"PIECES OF GOLD"

What I found on board astounded me. The ship had been ransacked. The two sailors who should have been on watch were lying on the deck. They had been severely beaten and one of them was dead! The other, Hands, had fainted. He had a large gash on his thigh. I gave him a sip of water to revive him.

Once he had recovered his senses, I explained that I wanted to sail the ship to the north of the island, and then run her aground. He listened attentively, and then replied, "Without me, you'll not be able to steer the ship on course. I can help you, but in exchange you must feed and take care of me. After all, I can't harm you; I can hardly walk." This appeared to be true, and so I accepted his proposal.

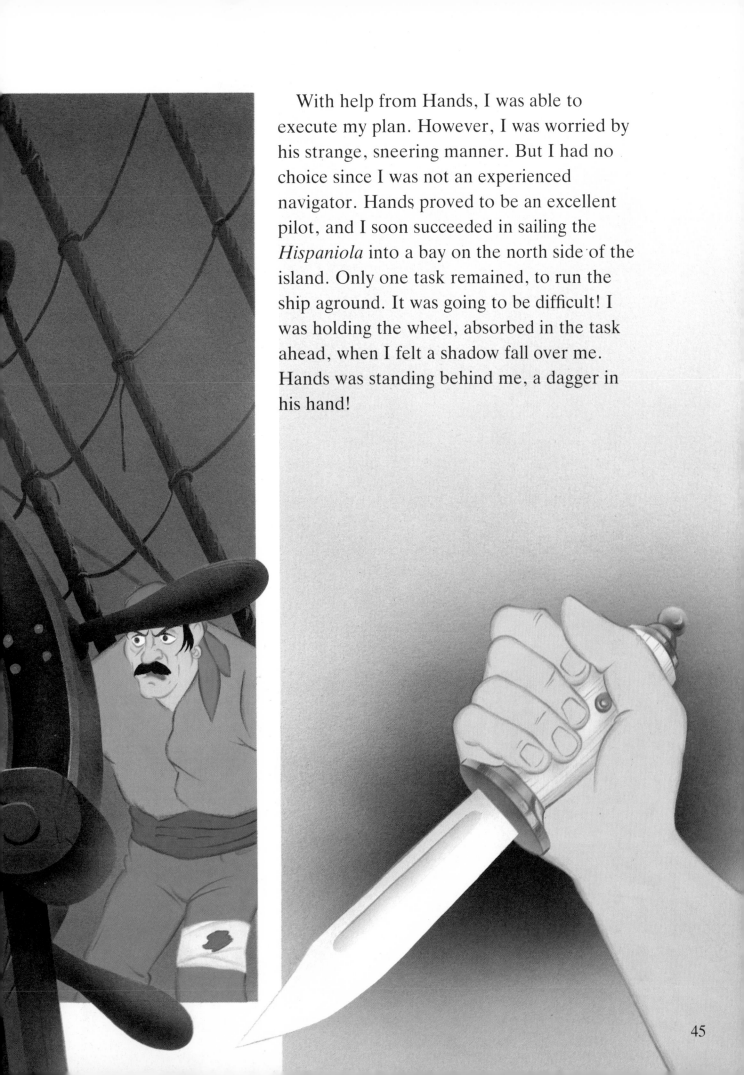

With help from Hands, I was able to execute my plan. However, I was worried by his strange, sneering manner. But I had no choice since I was not an experienced navigator. Hands proved to be an excellent pilot, and I soon succeeded in sailing the *Hispaniola* into a bay on the north side of the island. Only one task remained, to run the ship aground. It was going to be difficult! I was holding the wheel, absorbed in the task ahead, when I felt a shadow fall over me. Hands was standing behind me, a dagger in his hand!

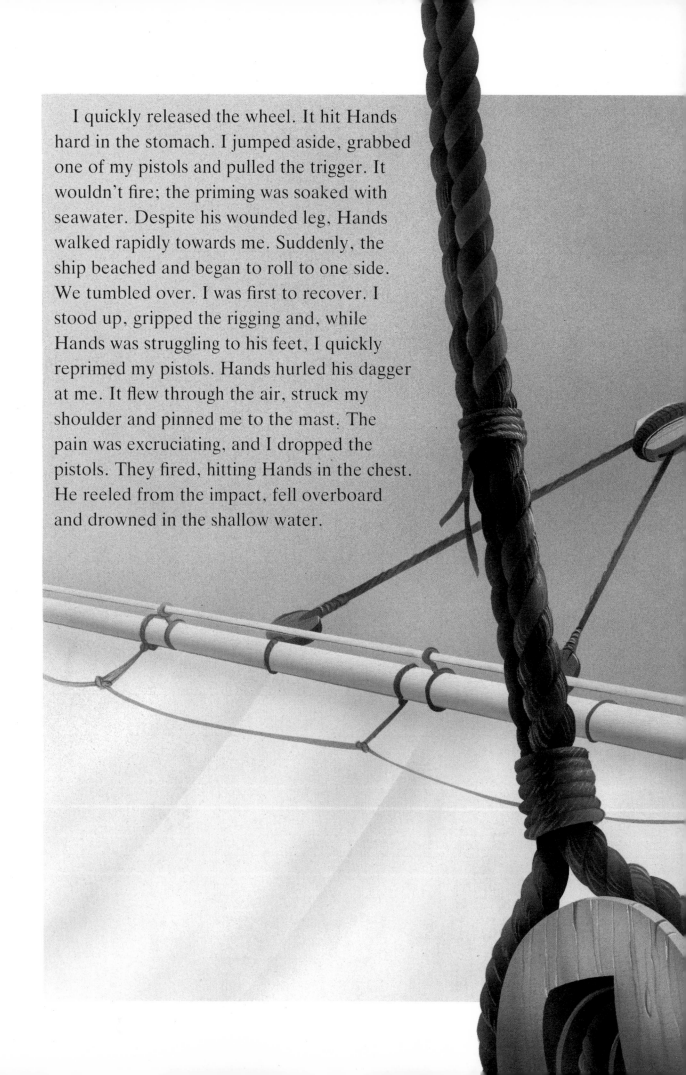

I quickly released the wheel. It hit Hands
hard in the stomach. I jumped aside, grabbed
one of my pistols and pulled the trigger. It
wouldn't fire; the priming was soaked with
seawater. Despite his wounded leg, Hands
walked rapidly towards me. Suddenly, the
ship beached and began to roll to one side.
We tumbled over. I was first to recover. I
stood up, gripped the rigging and, while
Hands was struggling to his feet, I quickly
reprimed my pistols. Hands hurled his dagger
at me. It flew through the air, struck my
shoulder and pinned me to the mast. The
pain was excruciating, and I dropped the
pistols. They fired, hitting Hands in the chest.
He reeled from the impact, fell overboard
and drowned in the shallow water.

Gently, I extracted the dagger from my shoulder and bathed the wound.

To save the ship, I dropped the sails. Then, I slid the length of the hull, reached the shore and made for the fort. An enormous bonfire had been lit. How strange! But all was quiet. I could even hear snoring. Where was the man on watch? I entered the fort, and, in the half light, bumped into a barrel. In the darkness, a shrill voice screeched, "Pieces of gold, pieces of gold!" It was Long John Silver's parrot, Captain Flint. The fort had fallen to the mutineers! I turned to escape, but too late! I was Long John Silver's prisoner. . . .

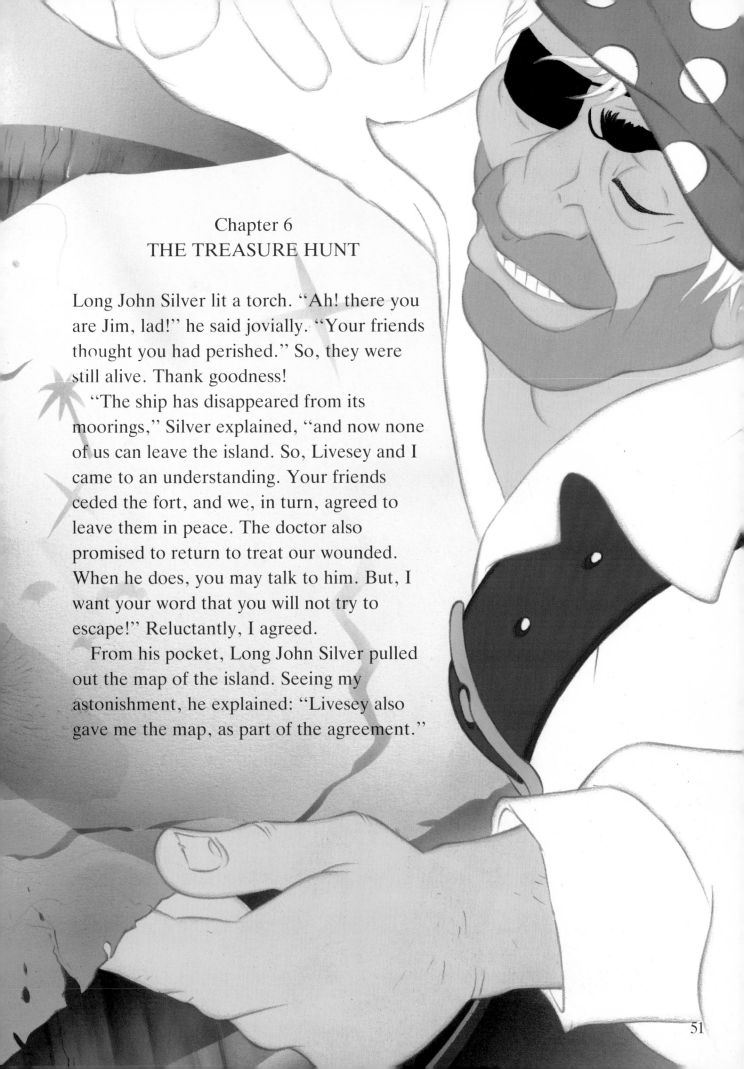

Chapter 6
THE TREASURE HUNT

Long John Silver lit a torch. "Ah! there you are Jim, lad!" he said jovially. "Your friends thought you had perished." So, they were still alive. Thank goodness!

"The ship has disappeared from its moorings," Silver explained, "and now none of us can leave the island. So, Livesey and I came to an understanding. Your friends ceded the fort, and we, in turn, agreed to leave them in peace. The doctor also promised to return to treat our wounded. When he does, you may talk to him. But, I want your word that you will not try to escape!" Reluctantly, I agreed.

From his pocket, Long John Silver pulled out the map of the island. Seeing my astonishment, he explained: "Livesey also gave me the map, as part of the agreement."

The doctor, as promised, came the next day to treat the wounded. When we were alone, I told him about the *Hispaniola* – he was delighted. Livesey begged me to return with him, but I had given my word to Silver. The doctor sadly left alone.

I was dragged along when Silver and his men left the fort and set off to find the treasure. They were excited, laughing and joking along the way, until they saw, at the base of a tree, a skeleton, with its long bony fingers pointing in the direction of the treasure. Despite the hot day, we all began to shiver. Then, in the distance, we heard a voice chanting Flint's song.

"*Fifteen men on the dead man's chest . . .*"

"It's the old pirate's ghost! Let's turn back!" cried one of the pirates.

"Come on, you cowards," bullied Silver. "It is not far now to the treasure, and soon you'll all be rich men."

The pirates became surly. Gone was their former excitement. The sight of the skeleton and the sinister chant had left them nervous and sullen. When we arrived at the spot where the treasure had been buried, we found nothing but a large hole in the ground and an *empty* chest! The gold had vanished!

The sailors were furious. I was standing next to Long John Silver when, swearing and cursing, they charged at us. Silver swiftly turned coat. He offered me a pistol, then started firing on his own men. I heard other shots. Doctor Livesey and Ben Gunn came running to our rescue. The mutineers fled. Long John Silver, alone, remained. He had saved my life!

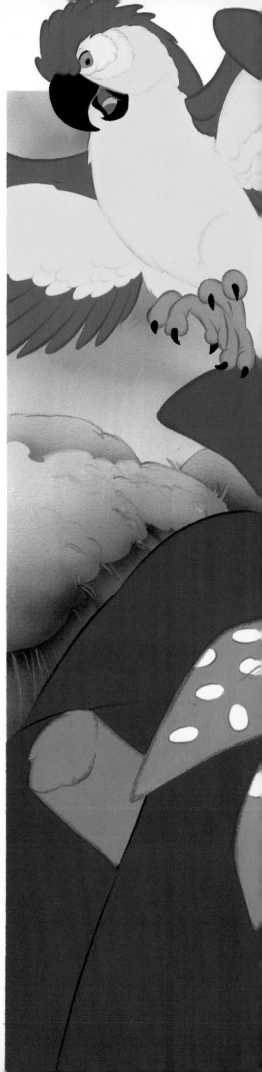

In return, Doctor Livesey protected Silver from Trelawney's and Smollett's wrath. We found them sheltering in Ben Gunn's cave, and piled high nearby was Flint's treasure! Ben Gunn had found it, by chance, during his three years alone on the island. Doctor Livesey had discovered this fact when he'd left the fort to find the castaway. Now I understood why he had given the map to Silver. It was, after all, useless!

And the sinister chanting that had scared us was simply Ben Gunn imitating the voice of old Captain Flint!

It took us several days to collect provisions and carry all Flint's treasure to the ship, which had now been refloated. Once the gold was loaded, we set sail, accompanied by Ben Gunn and Long John Silver. The mutineers were abandoned to their fate on the island.

The return journey was hard. A ship the size of the *Hispaniola* needed a large crew, and we had but a few experienced seamen. Long John Silver resumed his role as cook, but did not remain with us for long. One dark night, when we put into port for provisions, he slipped away, taking with him a sack of gold from our precious cargo. We never heard from him again.

Back in England, we divided Flint's treasure equally between us. I, Jim Hawkins, was rich beyond my wildest dreams. Captain Smollett retired, never to sail the high seas again, and Ben Gunn spent his fortune within a couple of weeks. Squire Trelawney became famous throughout the land for his tales of our adventures, and Doctor Livesey returned to his quiet country practice.

Many years have now passed since our adventure, but I have never forgotten my father's tavern, and the old buccaneer, Captain Bill.